THE BABY-SITTERS CLUB

™

Adapted by M.J. Carr
From THE BABY-SITTERS CLUB MOVIE
Based on the best-selling series
by Ann M. Martin

SCHOLASTIC INC.
New York   Toronto   London   Auckland   Sydney

ISBN 0-590-60405-8

The Baby-sitters Club Movie © 1995 Beacon Communications
Corp. and Columbia Pictures Industries, Inc.
Text copyright © 1995 by Scholastic Inc.
Photographs copyright © 1995 by Beacon Communications Corp.
and Columbia Pictures Industries, Inc.
All rights reserved. Published by Scholastic Inc.
THE BABY-SITTERS CLUB is a registered trademark
of Scholastic Inc.

12 11 10 9 8 7 6 5 4 3 2 1   5 6 7 8 9/9 0/0

Printed in the U.S.A.   37

First Scholastic printing, August 1995

Summer had arrived in Stoneybrook. It brought warm weather, softball games, and, of course, no school. For the seven members of the Baby-sitters Club, that meant more time for baby-sitting. The girls gathered in Claudia's bedroom for the first meeting of the summer.

Mary Anne and Dawn arrived together. They were stepsisters, and had become close friends. Jessi and Mallory, the two junior officers, cozied up on the rug. Kristy, the club president, called the meeting to order as Stacey ran in late.

"We have a crisis on our hands," announced Claudia. "I flunked science." Claudia was good at art but always had trouble in school. "If I don't get a C plus in summer school, I have to drop out of the club."

"I'll coach you," Kristy assured her. Just then, the phone rang. "Baby-sitters Club," she answered. Kristy was ready for business. The meeting was under way.

Stacey signed up for a job at the Wilders'. When she showed up to sit for Rosie, Rosie's cousin from Switzerland was there as well. He wasn't a little boy, as Stacey had expected. He was a handsome seventeen-year-old named Luca. Stacey had grown up in New York City, but Luca was even more sophisticated than she. Stacey was smitten.

"Thanks for helping me baby-sit," Stacey said, blushing.

"Why don't you show me around Stoneybrook?" Luca asked. "How about Saturday?"

"Sure," said Stacey. She fumbled self-consciously as she opened the door.

"I'll ring you!" Luca called after her.

At the next meeting of the Baby-sitters Club, Kristy announced, "I have a brilliant idea." She suggested that the girls start a day camp that would run through the summer.

"*This* brilliant idea might really be brilliant!" cried Jessi.

All the girls agreed. Dawn and Mary Anne had an idea of their own. They hoped they could hold the camp in the big yard around their farmhouse.

The girls trooped off to survey the yard. Kristy marked off an area that would be good for sports. Claudia searched for a shaded area to set up arts and crafts. Jessi found the perfect spot for dancing.

Now it was time to drum up kids for the camp. The girls scattered around town to post their fliers.

On the first day of camp, kids streamed up to the registration table. All of the girls' favorite kids were there — Rosie Wilder, Suzi Barrett, and Kristy's little brother, David Michael. Kristy wore a cap that said "Boss," and she shouted instructions through a megaphone. She divided the kids into groups and handed out colored potholders so the sitters could tell the groups apart.

Two boys arrived. One was Logan, Mary Anne's boyfriend and a fellow sitter. He'd come to help. His friend Alan Gray offered to work, too. The girls thought Alan was a dweeb. He acted more like a kid than many of the campers.

Kristy considered Alan's offer. "You can be a trainee," she agreed.

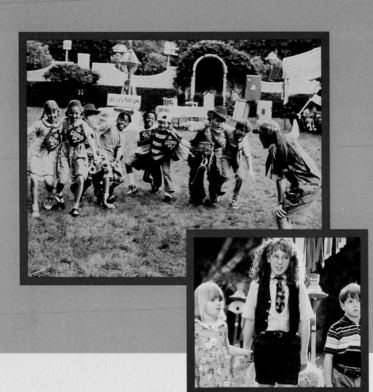

It seemed that the girls had everything under control. Kristy's group was running races.

"I have to go to the bathroom!" cried one of her campers.

Kristy stopped short. "Bathroom?" Oh, no! The Porta Potties hadn't arrived! Mary Anne's father didn't want the campers using the house, but the girls had no choice. They snuck the campers one by one through the back door to take them to the bathroom.

The girls didn't realize that someone was watching them. Cokie Mason, their sworn enemy, was hiding in the bushes with two friends. Cokie surveyed the cheerful bustle of activities at the day camp. A sneer crossed her face.

"Ladies," she declared to her friends, "we could do some major damage here."

That afternoon, Kristy and Mary Anne took a bicycle ride. Kristy heard someone call her name and turned to see who it was. "Dad?" she said, surprised. Before her stood her father, Patrick. He'd moved out of town years ago. Kristy hadn't seen him since she was six years old.

"I may be getting a job in town," he explained.

"Did you see Mom?" Kristy asked.

"I don't want her to know I'm here until I find out about the job," said Patrick. "Think we could keep it between us for a couple of days?"

Kristy's father got into his camper van and waved as he drove off. Kristy watched him, shaken.

The next day, camp was in full swing. Dawn helped her kids plant seeds in egg cartons. Kristy coached a softball team.

"Look alive out there," she shouted to her players who were sitting down in the field. Jackie Rodowsky was up at bat. They didn't think he could hit the ball. Jackie took a ferocious swing and *smack*— he hit the tip of his toe. "Ow!" he cried.

As the day drew to a close, Kristy ducked out of camp early, taking Mary Anne with her. Kristy had plans to see her dad.

Patrick made dinner for Kristy and Mary Anne. "Mouse pancakes," he said, grinning. He unveiled a plate of pancakes, each shaped like a little mouse. "When Kristy was younger, this was the only thing she would eat."

"When are you going to call Mom?" Kristy asked.

"Soon," Patrick promised. "Hey, I've got a present for you," he said, changing the subject. He handed Kristy a box. In the box was a dress, perfect for a girl Kristy's age. Perfect for a girl who wore dresses, that is.

"It's nice," Kristy stammered. "For a dress."

That night, Mary Anne stayed at Kristy's house. The girls changed into their pajamas and looked through old photos of Kristy and her dad.

"You have to tell your mom that he's here," said Mary Anne.

"I can't," Kristy moaned miserably. "I promised. And you can't tell anyone, either."

When Kristy and Mary Anne had rushed off to meet Patrick, they left the rest of the Baby-sitters with the task of closing up camp for the day. When the girls had finished, Claudia and Dawn walked home together. On the opposite side of a neighboring yard, they discovered a greenhouse. It was run-down, deserted, and overgrown with weeds.

"This would make an amazing office for the club," Claudia suggested. "We could get the kids to help clean it up."

The next day after camp, the girls in the Baby-sitters Club loaded up wagons with cleaning supplies. Once again, Kristy snuck off early. She slipped into her dad's van.

"Who's that man?" asked Claudia.

"No one," Mary Anne blurted out.

The other girls looked at her.

"Since when do we keep secrets?" demanded Stacey.

"I can't tell," Mary Anne pleaded. "I promised."

Next to the field, a neighbor, Mrs. Haberman, was working in her garden.

Suddenly, a stink bomb landed in the center of her flowerbed. Cokie had hidden the stink bomb in the camp. Some of the kids had found it and hurled it over the hedge.

"Aaah!" screamed Mrs. Haberman. Then she walked over to the camp.

"You look like decent, sensible girls," she said, "so we'll call this a warning. But if there's any more trouble, I'll call the city and report the camp!"

Cokie Mason and her friends were watching from behind the bushes. Cokie had an idea. If the Baby-sitters Club wanted to fix up the greenhouse, she could "fix" it, too.

That week, Stacey had a date with Luca. She paced her front hallway, waiting for him to arrive. "I hate what I'm wearing," she said nervously. "Should I change my socks?"

"Did you eat?" her mother prodded her. Stacey had diabetes. If she didn't eat regularly, she got dizzy and sick.

"I will before I go," Stacey promised.

Just then, the doorbell rang. It was Luca. He had slung a canteen over his shoulder and tied a bandanna around his neck. Luca had planned a hike. Before her mother could stop her, Stacey scooted out the door.

Luca led Stacey on a trail through the woods, then started up a steep hill. Stacey began to feel faint.

"I hear there's a fantastic view at the top," Luca said, tramping ahead.

Stacey tried to keep up, but her skin felt clammy. She was sweating through her clothes. Stacey was embarrassed and didn't want to tell Luca what was the matter.

"I've got to go," she said abruptly. She broke away from Luca and ran down the hill. When Luca caught up with her, she was slumped against a tree. "I need to eat something," she said weakly.

Luca pulled an apple out of his sack. As Stacey ate it, she explained about her condition.

"I wish you had told me," said Luca. "It's no big deal. I'm just glad you're better."

Before Stacey knew what was happening, Luca leaned toward her and kissed her.

Summer wore on. July turned to August. With each day, Kristy saw more and more of her dad. He took her to play softball. They had picnics. Each time she snuck off to visit him, she had to lie to her mother and her friends.

One afternoon, at a club meeting in Claudia's room, the girls waited for Kristy to join them. Kristy was late. By the time she arrived, the meeting had nearly ended. The girls were discussing the problem of Mrs. Haberman.

"Who's Mrs. Haberman?" Kristy asked.

"If you'd been around," Stacey said icily, "you would know."

The girls were fed up with Kristy. The day camp was in danger and Kristy — the president of the club — wasn't helping a bit! One by one the girls huffed out of the room. Kristy was left alone with Claudia.

"I heard you flunked a science quiz," said Kristy. "Sorry."

But Claudia was angry at Kristy, too. Kristy never had time to help her study, as she'd promised. And Claudia's final was coming up soon.

It seemed that everyone was angry at Kristy. Later that week, she once again slipped away from work early to meet her father. This time, she left her little brother at camp. She'd forgotten that she'd promised to bring him home. David Michael searched for Kristy. When he couldn't find her, he shrugged and headed down the busy road by himself. That evening, when Kristy got home, her mother and Watson, her stepfather, were waiting for her.

"I can't believe you let this happen," Watson said angrily. "What's gotten into you lately?"

"You wouldn't understand," Kristy replied.

"I'm your father," he persisted. "I want to know what's going on."

"You're *not* my father!" Kristy shouted. "Leave me alone!" She ran to her room and slammed the door.

Later, Kristy called Patrick on the phone. When she hung up, her family walked into the kitchen and found her crying.

"What's wrong?" asked her mother.

"I have an allergy " Kristy sniffed.

"What are you allergic to?" David Michael asked.

"Summer!" Kristy snapped.

Even though Kristy's friends were upset with her, they still planned a party for her birthday. The girls huddled together at day camp out of Kristy's earshot. Mallory had good news. Her parents had said they could have the party at her aunt's cabin near a lake.

Stacey announced her own news. Her mom had agreed to let her go to New York City for a weekend to show Luca the sights. She and Claudia could stay with Stacey's father, in his apartment. Claudia would be allowed to go, though, only if she passed her science final.

"If I fail my final my life is ruined," moaned Claudia.

"You won't fail," Mary Anne assured her.

As Claudia watched, the members of the club joined together in the barn and began clapping and stomping in rhythm. Kristy was front and center. She started up a rap, and the other baby-sitters joined in. They rapped about the heart. They rapped about the brain.

"The brain, the brain, the center of the chain," they chanted.

The words they made up were catchy. Claudia knew the rap would help her remember all the information she would need to know for her final.

When the dance ended, each of the girls stepped forward and handed Claudia her own, prized good luck charm. If all this didn't help her with the final, nothing would.

The days of summer were passing swiftly. Still, Kristy kept the secret about her father. At camp, the girls crowded around and finally confronted her.

"You're always leaving early!" Stacey accused her.

"What's up with you?" demanded Dawn.

Kristy couldn't tell her friends. She hadn't told anyone except Mary Anne, not even her mother. That afternoon, when she met her father at the ballpark, she let him know how she felt.

"Why'd you come back if you're just going to hide?" she asked.

"I came back to see you," said Patrick.

"You could have come before," Kristy said, her voice catching. "But you never did. You never even called." The words spilled out of her in a rush. "You don't care about me. I'm lying to everyone who *does* care, and it's your fault. I'm going to tell Mom you're here!"

Patrick persuaded Kristy to wait until her birthday. He promised her that he would take her to the amusement park to celebrate. "I'll pick you up at home," he said, "and we can tell everyone together."

"Really?" said Kristy.

"Absolutely," answered her dad.

Kristy hoped Patrick was telling the truth. That would be the best birthday present of all.

The next day, the members of the Baby-sitters Club gathered to work on the greenhouse. Kristy asked Logan and Alan to help out. The Stoneybrook Civic Committee was scheduled to inspect the building. Claudia arrived to help. She was grinning from ear to ear.

"I passed!" she cried. "I passed summer school!" The girls squealed and fell on her with hugs. Now Claudia could stay in the club *and* go on the trip to New York City!

When Stacey and Claudia arrived in New York, they met up with Luca and three of his friends. The group strolled around the trendy downtown streets, taking in the sights. Luca's friends were older and very sophisticated. Luca put his arm around Stacey.

"Stacey's only sixteen," he said to his friends. "A delicious sixteen."

Luca led the group to a club. When the bouncer at the door checked their ID's, he turned away Stacey and Claudia. Luca grabbed Stacey's ID and checked her birthdate.

"Thirteen!" he shouted. "You never told me you were thirteen!" Stacey's face turned red. Luca hustled Stacey and Claudia into a cab and rode back with them to Stacey's father's apartment. Luca was furious that she had lied. "This is a *really big* deal!" he shouted at her.

Stacey couldn't believe that Luca was so angry. "Jerk!" she shouted back.

Each day after camp, the members of the Baby-sitters Club continued to work on the greenhouse. Back at camp, two of the campers busied themselves planting some flowers in the ground. Dawn glanced at the big mound of blooms next to the kids. They had plucked them from Mrs. Haberman's garden!

Mrs. Haberman stomped over to the camp, spitting mad. "I've had enough!" she shouted. "I'm calling the city!" Before Dawn could answer, Mrs. Haberman stormed back home.

Dawn knocked on Mrs. Haberman's door,
hoping to make peace. Mrs. Haberman invited her
in and offered her tea. The flowers the kids had
picked had been imported from Africa and South
America. Dawn knew she could never replace them.

"I don't know how much more of your camp I can
take," Mrs. Haberman said with a sigh.

Mrs. Haberman was not the only threat to the day camp. Cokie and her friends had been busy with their nasty plot. They bought paint rollers and cans of paint, then lugged them to the greenhouse. When the campers had left for home and the greenhouse was deserted, the girls went to work. They splattered paint on the freshly cleaned walls. They stomped through the wet cement. Cokie turned to admire her dirty work. As she did, the pole of her roller swung around, too. It cracked a window, leaving a huge, gaping hole.

That day was Kristy's birthday. While the other girls prepared her party at the cabin, Kristy waited at home for her dad. He'd promised to pick her up, but he was late. Time passed. Kristy grew restless. She took a taxi to the amusement park and looked for him there. Her father was nowhere to be found.

As Kristy searched for Patrick, it started to rain. The other people in the park hurried toward the exits. Kristy found a phone and called her friends at the cabin.

Lightning flashed. Her phone call was cut off. The park was beginning to close. Kristy ran to leave the park, but the guard had already locked the gates. Tears welled in Kristy's eyes. Once again, her father had let her down. Kristy climbed over the fence and stood alone outside the park. She was shivering and cold.

At the cabin, Mary Anne finally told the others about Kristy and her dad. She told them Kristy was probably at the amusement park in the storm.

When her friends realized that Kristy was in trouble, they sprang into action. Stacey swallowed her pride and called Luca. She asked him to pick them up and drive them to the amusement park. At the park, the girls found Kristy just outside the gates. She looked up and saw the faces of her friends and ran into their arms. Luca drove the girls back to the cabin.

Stacey lingered a moment with Luca. "Thanks for helping," she said awkwardly.

Luca smiled. He wasn't angry any longer, either.

"I'm coming back next summer," he said. He leaned over and kissed Stacey one last time before she ran to join her friends.

At long last, Kristy was able to tell the girls everything about her father. Her friends bundled her in blankets and sat her in front of a roaring fire. Jessi and Mallory marched in with Kristy's birthday cake. It was an ice cream cake, and by this time had half melted away.

"Make a wish!" they chorused.

Kristy smiled. She pulled the blankets tighter and blew out the candles. Her birthday was happy after all.

When Kristy got home, she told her mother the truth as well.

"I could wring Patrick's neck for doing this to you," her mother said, shaking her head.

"Why is he like that?" Kristy asked.

Her mother sighed. "Oh, honey," she said, "your dad is fun, but he promises to do a lot of things he doesn't do."

A letter had come for Kristy in the mail. She tore it open. It was a good-bye letter from Patrick. He told her that the job hadn't worked out after all, and that he was taking off for Colorado. "Remember," he wrote, "I owe you a ride on The Monster."

Kristy's mom gave her a big, warm hug.

"Your dad's full of dreams, baby," she said to comfort her. "So are you and that's not bad."

When the members of the Baby-sitters Club arrived at the greenhouse, they were shocked. Cokie had done her damage. The greenhouse was a big, wet, globby mess.

"The civic committee is coming tomorrow!" cried Mary Anne.

Kristy and Claudia took charge. They organized the sitters into cleaning crews. By the time the committee arrived, the greenhouse fairly sparkled.

Mrs. Haberman arrived with the others. The girls hadn't known she was on the committee. Surely she'd vote against their plans.

But she surprised everyone. "The girls have worked hard," she argued. "They deserve to use the greenhouse as an office."

The committee agreed with Mrs. Haberman. After they announced their decision, they loosened their collars and rushed out for air. It was awfully hot inside the greenhouse, fine for plants but too hot for people.

The next meeting of the Baby-sitters Club was held in its usual spot, Claudia's room. The girls planned their move to the greenhouse.

"I'm going to miss it here," said Mary Anne.

"It's so nice and cool," Stacey said wistfully.

The girls looked at each other. No one really wanted a new office. They had an idea.

The next day, the sitters and campers paraded to the greenhouse. They had their wagons in tow, this time filled with pots of flowers and long flats of seedlings. Dawn ran to get Mrs. Haberman. "It's all yours," Dawn explained. She gestured to the greenhouse and grinned widely.

"We thought you could use it to grow all your flowers and stuff," Kristy chimed in.

Mrs. Haberman was touched and thrilled. She waved the kids together.

"Group shot!" Mrs. Haberman said as she focused her camera.

Everyone crowded in close. Each of the girls in the club had had a fun, eventful summer. They had learned things from the day camp and from their friends. Around them, the first leaves of autumn were falling.

"Say 'Trees,'" Mrs. Haberman cried out.

"Trees!" everyone shouted.

The girls linked their arms around each other and beamed broadly. Mrs. Haberman snapped the picture. Summer in Stoneybrook had drawn to a close.